nickelodeon

THAT GIRL
Lay Lay

BUST
YOUR OWN
RHYMES

...AND
DISCOVER THE
STAR YOU ARE!

By Terrance
Crawford

SCHOLASTIC INC.

All rights reserved. Published by Scholastic Inc., *Publishers since 1920.* SCHOLASTIC
and associated logos are trademarks and/or registered trademarks of Scholastic Inc.

The publisher does not have any control over and does not assume any responsibility
for author or third-party websites or their content.

This book is a work of fiction. Names, characters, places, and incidents are either the
product of the author's imagination or are used fictitiously, and any resemblance to
actual persons, living or dead, business establishments, events,
or locales is entirely coincidental.

978-1-338-77962-2 (Trade ISBN)

978-1-338-81448-4 (Book Fairs ISBN)

10 9 8 7 6 5 4 3 2 1   22 23 24 25 26

Printed in China   68

First edition 2022

Background images © Shutterstock.com.

Book design by Becky James

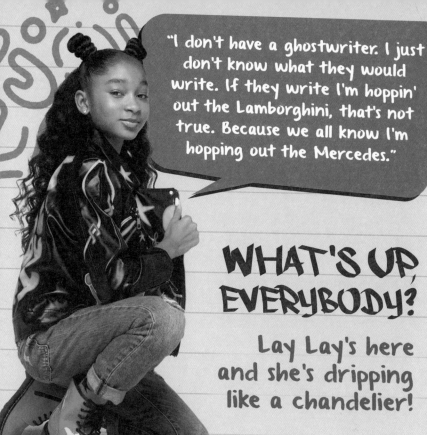

"I don't have a ghostwriter. I just don't know what they would write. If they write I'm hoppin' out the Lamborghini, that's not true. Because we all know I'm hopping out the Mercedes."

WHAT'S UP, EVERYBODY?

Lay Lay's here and she's dripping like a chandelier!

MEET THAT GIRL LAY LAY. She raps, she sings, she dances, and she's poised to take over the world! While you may not be able to ghostwrite Lay Lay's lines for her, using the prompts in this book, you'll be able to bust rhymes, kick lyrics, and spit fire just like she does. What are you waiting for? Your journey to hip-hop superstardom starts **HERE!**

You probably know a whole lot about Lay Lay, like that her birthday is January 28 and she's been rapping since the age of five. So now tell Lay Lay some things about *you*!

My name is **Elliot**

I am **9** years old

I live in **Indanapilos**

My favorite solo artist is **lizzo**

My favorite band is **Julie and the Phantoms**

My favorite rapper is **lay lay**

I LIKE TO:

● dance ○ sing ○ rap

○ sleep ○ eat ○ cook ○ read ● play

● joke ○ juggle ○ paint ○ perform

○ race ● shop ○ wander ○ write

○ other _____

> "I'm from Houston, so you know we supersize everything. When it comes to food, jewelry, cars, whatever —we always supersize it."

You know we gotta rep H-Town all day! Houston, Texas, is home to some of the tastiest food, the coolest people, and, of course, ya girl Lay Lay!

Where are you from? KunKey

How long have you lived there? 3 years

My favorite thing about my hometown is ??? I Don,t Know I Din.t live there long enhgoe.

The best kept secret in my town is I Don,t Know

Every girl boss and aspiring young MC needs a dope crew to kick it with. On tour and in school, Lay Lay's crew is always right by her side. Whether you're giggling at sleepovers or rehearsing together for the talent show, it's always good to have a talented team backing you up.

 # WHO ARE YOUR BEST FRIENDS?

My best friends are _Elise, nora, luse, Ayla_

and _BlalKey piper_

Their nicknames are _toilet piper,_

and _leise_

Our favorite things to do together are _talk,_
sing, gymnastic.

Like any good girl group or budding boy band, every group of friends needs a name—especially if you're going to be performing together. Your group's name is what people will know you by far and wide. What do you call your group of friends? Come up with a dope name for your crew. Then use the space below to design a logo for your group.

We call ourselves:

> "We rap about all types of things. Food, pots and pans, butterflies . . . It don't even matter; we just rap."

WHAT IS FREESTYLING?

A lot of people think that freestyle rapping is completely improvised, meaning that you come up with all your rhymes and lyrics on the spot. While some freestyle bars do come "off the dome," the real definition is a rhyme that's not about any particular subject and doesn't follow a particular style. Freestyles don't even have to tell a story—they can be looser . . . more, well, free!

Use the space below to write out a list of random things you could include in your freestyles.

food

pots and pans

butterflies

hearts

freinds

store (shoping)

cars

shcool

sleep over

FREESTYLIN'

SOME TIPS AND TRICKS TO ROCK A RHYME

Even the best rappers in the world started out by working on their craft. Luckily, they've shared their knowledge, making your climb to superstardom just a little bit easier. Use the tips below, and before you know it, you'll be busting with the best of them.

DON'T WORRY ABOUT RHYMING EVERY LINE EVERY TIME. The most important part is keeping the flow. The rhymes will come in time.

USE YOUR ENVIRONMENT. Including what's around you in your rhymes proves to everyone that you're actually spitting off the dome and it improves your improv skills.

COMMIT THE GOOD BARS TO MEMORY. If you're freestyling and you spit something hot, don't be afraid to write it down. You might be able to use it again later!

SWITCH UP YOUR BEATS. It's important to be able to adapt to any beat that comes your way, so be sure to switch up your backing track every once in a while.

"FILLER" UP! Don't be afraid to drop in a "filler bar," aka those backup lines that you've already written. They'll give you time to think if you're ever stuck for your next bar.

PRACTICE MAKES PERFECT. All you need to practice freestyling is you, so practice writing and performing your freestyles whenever you can!

That Girl Lay Lay has been rapping since she was five years old, riding in her dad's car, and she loves a good passenger-seat freestyle. Craft your own rhymes by filling in the blanks below. Then try performing your new freestyle for your friends!

we stay srong we _____ don't play

_____ come on come on come my way

yay you know it,s _____ pay day

_____ that,s the only time we gon' play

cusee it,s fridg nigt with _____ hot fries

_____ my eyes

WHAT IS A REMIX?

A remix is when an artist takes an existing track and transforms it into something different. This can mean anything from adding a new verse to changing the song's whole structure. Create your own remixes by putting a new spin on some of Lay Lay's most popular songs. Using the song title below as a prompt, write down whatever comes to mind for your track.

"RICH"

como dack

Lay Lay honed her freestyle skills by watching her dad. But when she wants to spit a verse off the dome, she often just listens to her own musical heroes for inspiration. Remembering how other artists' music makes her feel can sometimes be just what Lay Lay needs to jump-start her own creativity.

Who are a few artists who inspire you? How were you introduced to them? What about them do you find inspiring? Write all about them here!

YOU CAN GET WITH THIS, OR YOU CAN GET WITH THAT

Now, y'all know your girl Lay Lay would love to have it all, but every now and then we come across situations where we can choose only one option. Read the choices below and circle which *you* would prefer.

WOULD YOU RATHER . . .

Put ketchup on your fries **OR** put special sauce on your fries?

Stream the album **OR** see the concert live?

Have your lip gloss poppin' **OR** keep those edges laid?

Write a verse **OR** perform off the dome?

See your face on the TV **OR** hear your voice on the radio?

Be super-rich **OR** world-famous?

Have a private plane **OR** a personal driver?

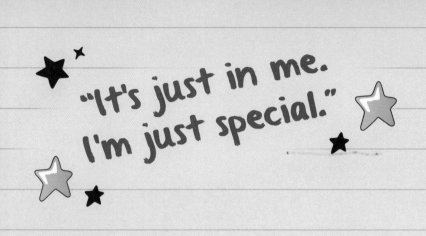

Lay Lay is one of the busiest people around. Between school and the studio and her hobbies like yoga, dancing, and gardening, she always has something to do! What does your daily schedule look like? Use this page to keep track of your day and see how it compares to Lay Lay's!

7:00 AM	stretching
8:00 AM	yoga
9:00 AM	breakfast
10:00 AM	youtube
11:00 AM	play
12:00 PM	school
1:00 PM	freinds
2:00 PM	eat (snuck)
3:00 PM	makeup
4:00 PM	studio time
5:00 PM	Dinner
6:00 PM	youtude
7:00 PM	Good night

Ya girl Princess Slaya has a full plate. But she always finds time to squeeze in her schooling, even when she's on the road!

What is your favorite subject? recus

What do you like about it? you don,t have to lenrn

Who is your favorite teacher? miss curry

What makes this teacher so special? She tuhct me stuff

What was the most fun you ever had at school?

one of them is. when we hada party.

What do you want to do with your life? Do you want to perform at the Macy's Thanksgiving Day Parade? Rap with your favorite celebrities? Use this space to write out some of your short-term goals (like passing your next math test) and your long-term goals (like getting into college or winning a Grammy!).

MY SHORT-TERM GOALS ARE:

1. to do in gymnactic
2. to succeed in 4th grade
3. Learn pihou
4. get acryile nails (Real)

MY LONG-TERM GOALS ARE:

1. to get a hous with stains
2. to meet zak eepoe
3. become a uckriss
4. get a 1,000 doavlls

A big part of making your dreams come true is working hard. What is your biggest dream and what can you do to help make it happen? Use this space to write out some ideas for accomplishing your goals, just like Lay Lay!

Well I want to be a actriss.
I could go to a drma clup. and
get into othen stuff and
fulten for plays.

RHYME TIME

Do all freestyles have to rhyme? No way! But rhyming is an easy way for beginners to learn structure and tempo—not to mention rhyming is just plain fun. Test your skills by coming up with as many rhymes for the following words as you can. To challenge yourself even more, try setting a timer first!

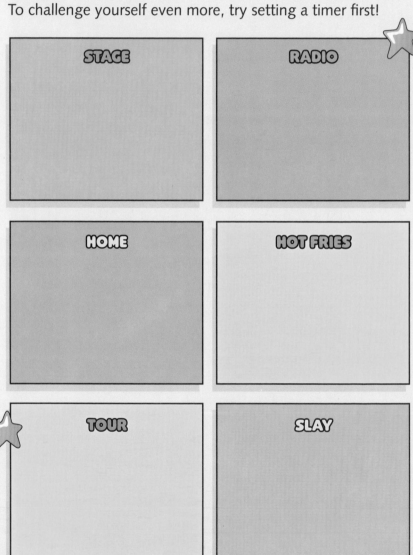

STAGE

RADIO

HOME

HOT FRIES

TOUR

SLAY

Lay Lay loves listening to her favorite songs and artists when she's getting ready for a big performance. What are some of your favorite tracks? Create a playlist in the spaces below that never fails to get you **hype**!

PLAY

TITLE | ARTIST

"Go Lay Lay Go" | That Girl Lay Lay

Imagine that you just scored your first record deal! But the studio needs you to make a lot of decisions before you can start sharing your music with your fans.

What kind of music would you make for your album?

_____

_____

_____

_____

_____

A feature is when one artist lends their talent to another artist's track, almost like a "guest star" on a TV show.

Who would you ask to feature on your album?

_____

_____

_____

_____

_____

_____

Using the blanks below, fill in some song titles for your album to create the track list.

_____

_____

_____

_____

_____

_____

_____

_____

_____

_____

Next, you need to come up with a design for your album. Use the space below to draw the album's cover art. Don't forget to include your name and the album's title, too!

"As soon as I touch that mic, I'm ready to turn up onstage. There's no going back."

> "Oh, trust me, [I'm not missing out].
> I have a whole sleepover planned. Music,
> pizza . . . yeah, just me and the girls!"

Imagine that you are throwing the wildest sleepover ever, just like Lay Lay did in the music video for her song "Slumber Party." What are you going to need? Who are you going to invite? And which of your friends is going to fall asleep first?

List five friends to invite to your slumber party:

That Girl Lay Lay
_____   _____

_____   _____

_____   _____

What are you bringing to the party?

CHECKLIST

- ○ **sleeping bag**   ○ **extra pillows**
- ○ **extra blankets**   ○ **snacks**   ○ **pajamas**
- ○ **bumpin' playlist**   ○ **playing cards**
- ○ **nail polish**   ○ **movies**
- ○ **other** _____

REMIX

Remixes are versions of songs that have been changed to sound different from the original. Create your own remix to one of Lay Lay's classic tracks by freestyling a verse in the space provided. Use the song title as a prompt to get you started!

"SLUMBER PARTY"

"The more you go higher, the more people try to bring you low, and you just can't let them do that."

Lay Lay knows the importance of surrounding yourself with people who have good energy. What qualities do you think are important for a person to have? Is it important that people are kind, or funny, or smart? Write about these qualities here and the people in your life who have them.

After your album comes out, imagine that you and your crew are going on a national tour. You get to perform in some of the coolest arenas all around the country!

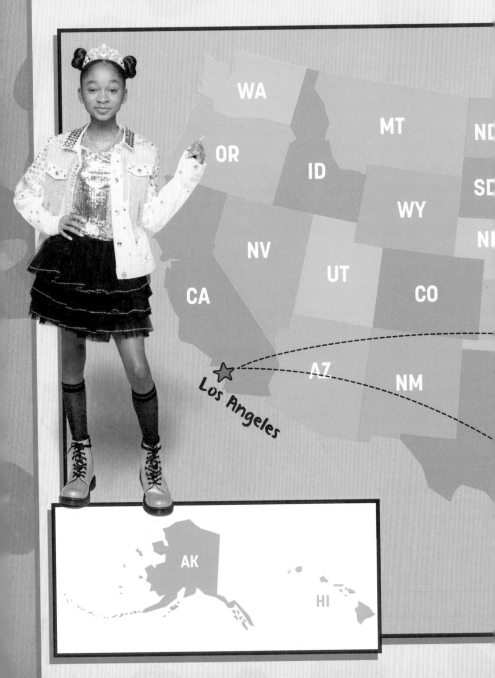

Would you stop in Lay Lay's hometown of Houston, Texas? What about the Universal Hip-Hop Museum in the Bronx, New York? Use the map below to plot out your nationwide tour!

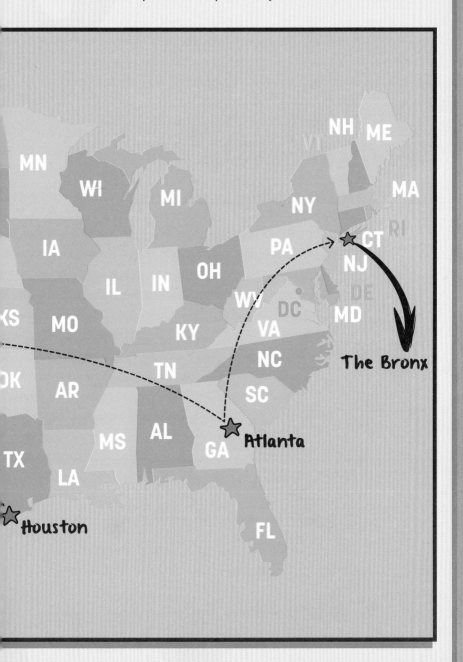

You are the star of your dream concert. Who's in the crowd? Where would you insert the showstopping dance break? Answer the questions below to plan your big show.

My opening night venue is _____

My opening act would be _____

I warm up the crowd with _____

The song that brings them to their feet is

_____

I'LL NEED MY PEOPLE TO BRING:

★ CHECKLIST

○ a fog machine   ○ fireworks

○ laser lights   ○ extra speakers

○ suspicious amounts of confetti

○ inflatable beach balls   ○ a T-shirt cannon

○ other _____

_____

The song I perform when they beg for an encore is _____

_____

Now write out how you imagine the whole night plays out!

_____

_____

_____

_____

_____

_____

_____

_____

_____

_____

_____

_____

_____

What drew the big crowds to your concert? Use the space below to draw a flyer for your tour. Don't forget to include the name of your big show!

REMIX

It's time for another remix! Put your own unique spin on FatCat's "Options" like That Girl Lay Lay did when she featured on the song. Kick things off by finishing the lyrics started for you below!

"OPTIONS"

When we walk into the room

Man, there ain't no stoppin' us

Because you know we got options

Have you ever been to a concert? Who was performing? How was it different from hearing the artist on the radio or streaming their songs online? What was your favorite part of the concert? Write all about that memory here. Or, if you haven't been to a concert yet, write about who you would like to see if you had the opportunity to go!

YOU CAN GET WITH THIS, OR YOU CAN GET WITH THAT

Even That Girl Lay Lay can't always have it all. Read the choices below and circle which *you* would prefer if you had to choose.

WOULD YOU RATHER . . .

Pull up in the drop top OR **cruise by in the low rider?**

Have ice on your neck OR **cash in your hand?**

Wear the freshest shoes OR **have the flyest 'do?**

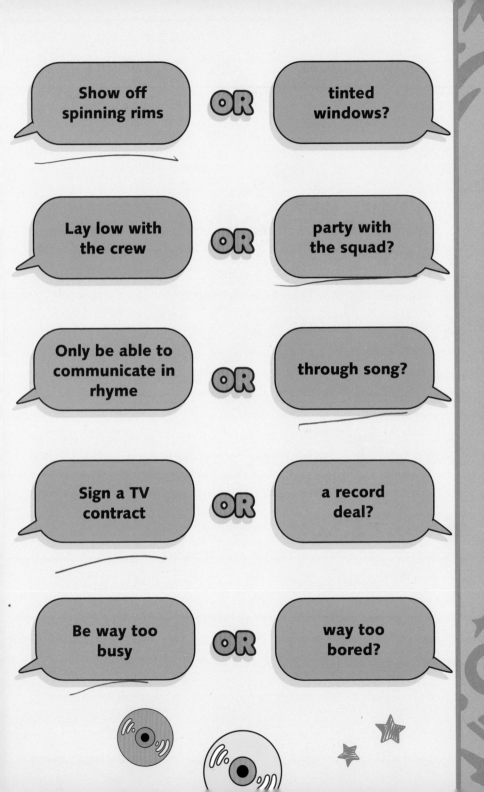

When Lay Lay isn't tearing it up onstage or at school, she likes to kick it with her friends, garden, and dance.

What are some of your favorite hobbies?

I LIKE:

- ● dancing
- ○ singing
- ○ rapping
- ● skating
- ○ sleeping
- ● playing video games
- ○ reading
- ○ watching TV
- ● playing sports
- ○ cooking
- ● baking
- ○ drawing
- ○ texting
- ○ exercising
- ● swimming
- ○ shopping
- ● volunteering
- ○ other _____

REMIX

A good remix takes the best parts of the original and adds a dash of something new. Put your own unique spin on Lay Lay's "Breezy" by writing an original verse below.

"BREEZY"

"If you can't catch up with me, go ahead and just sit this one out, homeboy."

Rap allows people to express themselves through rhyme. Part of the appeal of freestyling is that performers can go off the dome and rap about what's going on around them in real time. Look around the room and list five things that you could freestyle about right now.

1. _____

2. _____

3. _____

4. _____

5. _____

You can also freestyle about other things happening in your life. List three things that you've got coming up soon. It could be a family vacation that you're excited for, a math test that you're worried about, or just a TV show that you plan on watching tonight.

1. _____

2. _____

3. _____

Using a couple items from your lists on the opposite page as inspiration, craft a brand-new freestyle in the space below.

_____

_____

_____

_____

_____

_____

_____

_____

_____

_____

_____

_____

_____

Flow check! Test your skills against Lay Lay's by completing the lines started for you below. Then practice your performance by singing your new lyrics to a friend or family member!

_____ ask for me

_____ bag for me

_____ high class for me

_____ just for me

On the way to _____

Feeling like _____

Got my _____ and my _____

I hope that I _____

REMIX

Because remixes use familiar tracks, they're a great way for an artist to create or grow their fan base. Give it a try by remixing Lay Lay's "Mama." Fill in the blank space below with your own lyrics for a cool new verse.

"MAMA"

Y'all know whenever That Girl Lay Lay steps out, she's got to look poppin'. That means hair done and steez on fleek. Who is your style icon? Write about them here, then draw some of their best looks on the next page. If you can, find pictures of them and tape or glue them in, too!

My style icon is _Julio, sky_

I love their style because _it sooooo_

much funcky stuff

it so cool

_____

If I could steal one item from their closet, it would be _t.shirt_

_____

One outfit that lives in my head rent-free is _??_

_?3_

_____

_____

STYLE

"If you know truly that you're good at something that you wanna do, then just keep going."

Everyone has done things that make them feel important, like scoring a game-winning point or answering a tough question in class. That's how Lay Lay felt when she became one of the youngest people ever to get a record deal with her label. Write about an accomplishment of yours and why it makes you feel proud.

Lay Lay is all about doing good and making a change. List five things in your life that are perfectly good as they are.

1.

2.

3.

4.

5.

Now list five things that could use some changing.

1.

2.

3.

4.

5.

Is there anything you can do to help change these things? Write some ideas in the space below.

_____

_____

_____

_____

_____

_____

_____

_____

_____

_____

_____

_____

_____

_____

"In school, I used to get bullied sometimes, but I never really let them bring me down."

That Girl Lay Lay has proved she's multitalented—from her performances at Legoland and Nickelodeon's Kids' Choice Awards to being the youngest female rapper signed to her label and even starring in her own TV show. She raps and sings, writes her own lyrics, dances, and acts. Lay Lay is definitely a triple threat!

Do you have one thing that you're really good at? Or are you more like Lay Lay, with interests in lots of different areas? Answer the questions below to find out what kind of performer you should be.

1. After school you can usually be found:
A. Hitting the high notes on the ride home
B. At practice for whatever sport is in season
C. Rehearsing lines for the school play
D. Jotting down ideas in your notebook

2. It's a rainy Saturday night. You're staying in with:
A. Your headphones and your favorite playlist
B. A new workout video or online dance class
C. A pile of snacks and your Netflix queue
D. Staying in? On a *Saturday*?

3. What is your main strength?

    A. I'm creative

    B. I'm graceful

    C. I'm confident

    D. I'm a quick thinker

4. What's something you wish you were better at?

    A. Staying focused—I get lost in my thoughts sometimes

    B. Relaxing—I just can't sit still!

    C. Sharing the spotlight

    D. Speaking up for what I believe in

5. Who are you sitting with in the cafeteria?

    A. The band kids

    B. The soccer team

    C. The cast of the spring musical

    D. I check out a new table every day!

6. Which of these is your biggest pet peeve?

    A. People who are overly critical

    B. People who can't stay on beat

    C. People with no sense of humor

    D. People who talk over you

MOSTLY As

You were born to write music! You're always in sync with what's poppin', and you're probably the only one in your friend group who can carry a tune.

MOSTLY Bs

You're a dancer, obviously! Poise. Grace. Skill. You embody all those characteristics, and you're not half bad on the dance floor.

MOSTLY Cs

You're an actor, of course! You were destined to light up the stage and screen. But, you know, don't get *dramatic* about it.

MOSTLY Ds

You're a superstar meant to share your talent with the world. What are you even doing taking this quiz? Get out there!

REMIX

When making a remix, even the song's genre can be changed. There are no limits to what you can do, so get creative! Use the space below to freestyle a new verse to one of Lay Lay's biggest hits. You can use the prompt to get you started—or try something totally fresh!

"STOP PLAYIN'"

If you want to play

you'd better play with . . . Me

> **"Follow your dreams, don't let anybody tell you, like, 'Girl, you not good at it,' or 'Boy, you not good at this.'"**

That Girl Lay Lay's life totally changed when she went viral and made it big. If the same thing happened to you, what would be the first thing you'd do? Write all about your dreams for becoming a star here!

But fame isn't everything. What is one thing that you don't have to be famous to do? What are some things that might be easier or more fun if you're *not* famous?

Lay Lay's real name is Alaya, but she goes by many names, including That Girl Lay Lay and Princess Slaya. Come up with your own Lay Lay–inspired nickname by using the chart below.

NAME 1: Birth Month

January	=	Doctor	**July**	=	MC
February	=	Young	**August**	=	Grandmaster
March	=	Bad	**September**	=	The Greatest
April	=	DJ	**October**	=	The Original
May	=	Baby	**November**	=	Old
June	=	Lil'	**December**	=	Kid

NAME 2: First Letter of First Name

A	=	Wild	**J**	=	Cool	**S**	=	Trouble
B	=	Young	**K**	=	Funky	**T**	=	Swaggy
C	=	Big	**L**	=	Wicked	**U**	=	Ultimate
D	=	Slick	**M**	=	Crispy	**V**	=	Frosty
E	=	Tuff	**N**	=	Fly	**W**	=	Cheesy
F	=	Bad	**O**	=	Real	**X**	=	Mischief
G	=	Savage	**P**	=	Fresh	**Y**	=	Silent
H	=	Loud	**Q**	=	Supreme	**Z**	=	Flashy
I	=	Money	**R**	=	Lawless			

NAME 3: First Letter of Last Name

A	=	Bopz	**J**	=	Beast	**S**	=	Menace
B	=	Kidd	**K**	=	Kickz	**T**	=	Dolla$
C	=	Pantz	**L**	=	Funk	**U**	=	Face
D	=	Baby	**M**	=	Bunny	**V**	=	Socks
E	=	Royalty	**N**	=	Eyes	**W**	=	Mac
F	=	Tiger	**O**	=	Monster	**X**	=	Dawg
G	=	Blowfish	**P**	=	Alien	**Y**	=	Boss
H	=	Grillz	**Q**	=	Rapper	**Z**	=	Trillionaire
I	=	Hypeman	**R**	=	Master			

Don't forget to come up with a logo for your new hip-hop persona. You can try something simple, like Lay Lay's double L monogram, or something big and graphic, like her graffiti-style name—or you can even have different logos for different moods! Whether it's sweet or street, make sure your logo represents YOU!

MY NICKNAME IS

NAME 1	NAME 2	NAME 3

Not all nicknames have to be stage names. Do you have a nickname you just use with your family or friends? What is it? Who gave it to you? How long have you had it? Write the history of your nickname here.

"I have to speak
about what I say,
what is real."

Lay Lay has lots of fans and friends, but her most important relationship is the one she has with her parents. They show their support by always being there for her when she needs them.

What are your parents like? What do they mean to you? Use these pages to write about a time when one or both of your parents showed up for you when you needed them.

Lay Lay's song "Mama" is all about listening to what your mom says. Even though Lay Lay is a big star, she's still a kid with rules to follow at home, too! What are three rules at your house that you have to follow?

1. _____

2. _____

3. _____

If you could create three new rules, what would they be? How would these new rules make your life easier?

1. _____

2. _____

3. _____

RHYME TIME

Time for some freestyle practice! Find as many rhymes for the below words as you can and write them down so you're ready for your next showdown. Set a timer for yourself for an extra challenge!

STYLE

STEEZ

ICE

KICKS

DANCE

GROOVE

"No hating on anybody, I love everybody . . . Anybody in the industry . . . Just, everybody out there."

A collaboration is when two artists work together to create something doper than the sum of its parts. (Think of Lay Lay and Paul Wall in "Sleigh Ridin.") Bumping and thumping that H-Town music is always more fun with friends. List five artists who you would like to collaborate with. What kind of songs would you sing together? (Don't forget to include That Girl Lay Lay!)

1. That Girl Lay Lay

2.

3.

4.

5.

REMIX

It's time for another remix! Put your own spin on Lay Lay's track "Move Like I Move" by adding a totally new verse. You can use the lines started for you below as inspiration or go off the dome.

"MOVE LIKE I MOVE"

Yeah, move like I move

Groove like I groove

Do it like I do it

When you're a performer like Lay Lay, sometimes you're in a different city every night! Between filming her Nickelodeon show in Los Angeles, record label meetings in New York, and her countrywide tours, That Girl Lay Lay is always on the move. Answer the questions below to keep track of some of your own travels.

List five places that you have enjoyed visiting.

1. _____

2. _____

3. _____

4. _____

5. _____

Which was your favorite? Why did you go there? Were you on vacation? Visiting family? _____

_____

What was special about this place? _____

_____

_____

_____

Y'all know Princess Slaya is all about the vibes—no bad vibes, only positive. Lay Lay is too blessed to be stressed. In fact, one of the phrases she lives by is "No Stress, Just Finesse."

What are a few of the words you live by? What do these words or phrases mean to you?

> "I knew I was talented when I turned two. My dad [saw] it, my mom [saw] it, everybody saw that I was just talented. I've always wanted to be an entertainer."

Lay Lay always knew that she was born to be a performer! What makes you unique and helps you stand out from the crowd? Are you using this superpower to make a name for yourself? To help others? Use these pages to write about a time you were grateful you're not like everybody else.

YOU CAN GET WITH THIS, OR YOU CAN GET WITH THAT

Even That Girl Lay Lay has to make tough choices sometimes. Read the options below and circle which *you* would prefer if you had to choose.

WOULD YOU RATHER . . .

Dance your butt off OR **sing your heart out?**

Perform on a big stage OR **show up on the big screen?**

Go on a world tour with your crew **OR** be a solo superstar?

Pop up in Atlanta **OR** touch down in Houston?

Spend the day shopping with the gang **OR** spend the night having a sleepover with the girls?

Watch the concert live **OR** catch the livestream from your couch?

Get to wear a brand-new outfit every day **OR** have someone do your hair and makeup every day?

Lay Lay is a proud Aquarius, which explains her expressiveness and originality! Even though she's a big star, it's fun to get input from even *bigger* stars. Use the chart below to uncover your zodiac sign. Then check your horoscope on the next spread!

JANUARY 20–FEBRUARY 18	AQUARIUS	♒
FEBRUARY 19–MARCH 20	PISCES	♓
MARCH 21–APRIL 19	ARIES	♈
APRIL 20–MAY 20	TAURUS	♉
MAY 21–JUNE 20	GEMINI	♊
JUNE 21–JULY 22	CANCER	♋
JULY 23–AUGUST 22	LEO	♌
AUGUST 23–SEPTEMBER 22	VIRGO	♍
SEPTEMBER 23–OCTOBER 22	LIBRA	♎
OCTOBER 23–NOVEMBER 21	SCORPIO	♏
NOVEMBER 22–DECEMBER 21	SAGITTARIUS	♐
DECEMBER 22–JANUARY 19	CAPRICORN	♑

My birthday is

ARUNP

My zodiac sign is

_____

One way that I am like this sign is that

_____

_____

_____

_____

_____

_____

Astrology is an ancient tool for understanding ourselves and the stars. In astrology, each planet has an "association." People who follow astrology—like Lay Lay—believe that your personality and characteristics can be influenced by where the planets were in the sky when you were born.

Read a little more about the qualities of each zodiac sign below and check out your horoscope. Are you anything like your sign?

AQUARIUS
Qualities: resilient, fearless, independent
Horoscope: The world is a rough place sometimes, but you're not scared. Hold your head high, even when it doesn't seem like the easiest thing to do.

PISCES
Qualities: generous, creative, emotional
Horoscope: That project you've been working on in your head? Now is the best time to get started on it.

ARIES
Qualities: passionate, motivated, confident
Horoscope: The next time an opportunity presents itself, be bold and go for it!

TAURUS
Qualities: smart, dependable, hardworking
Horoscope: Your friends know that they can count on you, but make sure they know *you* appreciate *them*, too!

GEMINI
Qualities: adaptable, outgoing, intelligent
Horoscope: Even though you can adapt to anything life throws at you, make sure you're taking advantage of the days when you can just chill!

CANCER

Qualities: loyal, protective, intuitive
Horoscope: You usually have a pretty good idea of what's going down around you, so trust your instincts!

LEO

Qualities: warm, passionate, dynamic
Horoscope: You know the feeling when you're excited about something and you want to tell everyone? Follow that instinct—your friends will be thrilled to know your good news!

VIRGO

Qualities: practical, sensible, loyal
Horoscope: You've got something important happening. The best way to approach it is to work smart, not hard.

LIBRA

Qualities: fair, social, clever
Horoscope: You have a strong sense of right and wrong. Make sure you praise people who are doing the right things and call out people who aren't.

SCORPIO

Qualities: brave, determined, honest
Horoscope: Don't worry about that big task coming up. If you take it step by step, there's no way you won't come out on top.

SAGITTARIUS
Qualities: optimistic, fair, intellectual
Horoscope: You always see the lip gloss as half full, not half empty. That attitude will get you far in life!

CAPRICORN

Qualities: ambitious, driven, honest
Horoscope: You usually take on a lot of responsibility, but remember, you can always share the load and ask your friends for help.

Lay Lay knows that hard work is everything, but at a certain point, you have to step back and let the Universe do her work. Write a letter to the Universe telling her what you'd like to see in your life. Who knows—maybe she'll even read it.

Dear Universe,

douise

Take this journal with you the next time you go outside and observe what's around you. Are you in the city? The country? Somewhere in between?

List five things that you see.

1. _____

2. _____

3. _____

4. _____

5. _____

List four things that you hear.

1. _____

2. _____

3. _____

4. _____

List three things that you smell.

1. _____

2. _____

3. _____

Using any combination of the things you listed on the opposite page, write an outdoor freestyle in the space below. Try to add some cool rhymes and filler bars that you've written on other pages, too!

_____

_____

_____

_____

_____

_____

_____

_____

_____

_____

Freestyling is all about creating rap that flows without worrying about the style. You should be able to drop in at the end of a line or the beginning of a verse without breaking a sweat. Test your freestyle chops by starting and finishing the lyrics below to create your own verses.

_____ **back and forth**

_____ **back for more**

_____**askin' for**

_____ **for sure**

They say go_____

I tell them _____

'Cause I'm_____

Lookin' like _____

REMIX

Sometimes an artist puts such a cool spin on a remix that it can turn out better than the original song! Switch up Lay Lay's song "Curve" by writing the lyrics you imagine fit with that title. Remember, it can be totally different from Lay Lay's original rhymes—so get creative!

"CURVE"

"I write everything, because it's a particular way I like to write my stuff."

Beyoncé. Rihanna. Britney. What's a great concert without a few showstopping outfit changes? Use the mannequins below to sketch the dopest outfits you can imagine for your world tour.

Whether she's rocking her Princess Slaya "Space Buns" and the hottest kicks or slaying during her latest TV appearance, Lay Lay has confidence for days.

List five things that you like about yourself.

1. _____

2. _____

3. _____

4. _____

5. _____

What is your favorite thing about yourself? What do you do that makes you feel good about yourself?

Use the space below to write about how awesome you are!

_____

_____

_____

_____

_____

_____

Everyone has moments when they feel they aren't good enough or days when they just feel down. Even Lay Lay admits that she sometimes gets jitters in front of a big crowd or wishes that she could have a redo on a performance.

Use this space to write the words that you need to hear on a bad day.

_____

_____

_____

_____

_____

_____

_____

_____

_____

_____

_____

In Lay Lay's show on Nickelodeon, *That Girl Lay Lay*, she plays an avatar from an app that magically comes to life to help her best friend, Sadie.

If your life was a TV show, what would the plot be? What celebrity cameo would bring the studio audience to their feet? And most importantly, who's singing your theme song?

Fill in the blanks below to help write the lyrics to your show's theme song. Then slot the words you came up with into the corresponding spaces on the next page to see how your theme song comes to life!

Action #1

Noun

Action #2

Family member

Type of food

Thing

Action #3

Activity

Title of your show

On Mondays, I _____d_____
ACTION #1

my _____
NOUN

On Tuesdays, I _____
ACTION #2

with my _____
FAMILY MEMBER

Every Wednesday I get_____
TYPE OF FOOD

Every Thursday I get_____
THING

And on Fridays, I just_____
ACTION #3

On Saturdays, I _____ always
ACTIVITY

But I get through my days, with my girl Lay Lay,
And I guess that's why they call it

_____
TITLE OF YOUR SHOW

Lay Lay loves to eat—even strange combinations like french fries with seafood sauce! She's a pescatarian and she knows how important it is to eat healthy. But as a person, she also just likes to eat what tastes good!

What is your favorite food? _____

_____

Who is the best cook that you know? _____

_____

What is a food that you love that you don't get to eat often? _____

What is a dish you'd love to learn how to make?

_____

Write down the recipe for your favorite food. If you don't know it, make one up!

_____

_____

_____

_____

_____

REMIX

Sometimes a remix feels like a totally different song. But other times, only pieces of the song have changed. Mix your own version of Lay Lay's "Cheat Code" by filling in her original lines with your own lyrics.

"CHEAT CODE"

Some might say _____

_____ with the flow

_____ cheat code!

In the game like _____

_____ like uh-oh!

Then it's time for _____

_____ that's trouble.

_____ on the double.

LIL BIG DRIPPA

"I used to play soccer and I kicked the ball in the wrong goal and started celebrating!"

We've all had those moments: times when you're so embarrassed you wish the world would swallow you up! What's a time you felt downright mortified or made a mistake you wished people hadn't seen? How did you get over what happened? Write all about it here. Don't worry, your secrets are safe with Lay Lay!

If you're ever feeling down or alone, music is a totally safe and healthy place to turn. People have been putting their pain, frustration, and sadness into song since music began. Create a playlist of songs that you listen to when you feel sad.

PLAY	♥

TITLE	ARTIST
♥	
♥	
♥	
♥	
♥	

Do these songs cheer you up? Do they make you even sadder? How do these songs help you get through your bad days? _____

_____

_____

_____

"When you do something you love, nothing can frustrate you."

RHYME TIME

Freestyles and other bars don't have to rhyme, but it's always a good idea to keep your skills sharp. Find rhymes to these music and hip-hop phrases. Then see if you can use them to inspire a new verse!

FLEEK

RAP

BEAT

RHYME

TIGHT

CHILL

Remixes let artists stamp their own style onto another person's track. They also allow the artist to experiment, develop, and enhance their sound, or try out something completely new! Try something different here by filling in some new lines for one of Lay Lay's classic songs.

"FLY AWAY"

Watch me _____

I'mma just _____

_____, yeah, just watch me take off

Take off to the _____

Fly away to the _____

There's _____ everywhere

_____ is all I see

I'm gonna _____

The life of a celebrity isn't all tour buses and grand openings. Some people spend so much time listening to Lay Lay and watching her on TV, they think they know her. Lay Lay is a superstar who loves her fans, but she's wants everyone to know she's just a normal person, too! What is something that you wish more people knew about *you*?

YOU CAN GET WITH THIS, OR YOU CAN GET WITH THAT

Lay Lay is presented with a million choices every day—from what to wear and how to style her hair to what flavor lip gloss to use. Now it's your turn to make some tough choices. Read the options below and circle which *you* would prefer if you had to choose.

WOULD YOU RATHER . . .

Have two million dollars **OR** two million Instagram followers?

Have every song go straight to the top of the charts **OR** get recognized everywhere you go?

Do a worldwide press tour for a movie do a stadium tour for your album?

Have your favorite celebrity's phone number your favorite celebrity's car?

Be on a magazine cover on a billboard?

Get invited to the hottest parties every week receive a royalty check for your music every month?

Deal with the paparazzi your parents?

"I take maybe like two days or one day to write it, because I'm really thinking of what I'm writing."

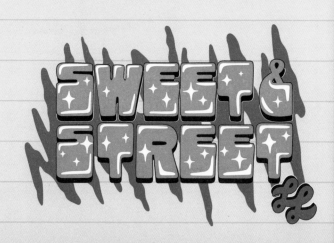

When Lay Lay hops out of bed in the morning, she's gotta look fly—from her hair to her feet. Use the space below to help Lay Lay secure the dopest kicks by sketching the freshest designs you can think of.

REMIX

When you see the song title "Supersize XL," what does it make you think of? A big meal? A movie monster? Something totally different?

If you know the lyrics to That Girl Lay Lay's version, is there anything you can think of that you would flip or change for the remix? Use the space below to write your take on what a song called "Supersize XL" would be. Get creative! This is *your* version.

"SUPERSIZE XL"

You wake up and have no school or responsibilities and an endless supply of money. What do you do on your perfect day?

I'm spending my perfect day with _____

_____

The first place we go is _____

When we get there, we _____

_____

_____

Next, we head to _____

so we can _____

The last thing we do on our perfect day is _____

_____

_____

_____

_____

_____

"My dream was to go viral and get signed. Guess it came true!"

When you're rapping without restrictions, the most important thing is your flow. That means being able to hop in and out of the lyrics while maintaining the beat. Fill in the blanks below, and get creative with your word choice. Then try performing your new verse for a friend to see how it flows.

_____ my wrist

_____ priceless

_____ dope

_____ new coat

All we do is _____ when we _____

They ask me _____

I tell them _____

REMIX

Imagine you get to add a verse to "I Need," just like Lay Lay did in her collab with Lil Tr33zy. What are some things you need? Try to incorporate at least four of them into your freestyle verse below.

"I NEED"

That Girl Lay Lay is all about family. She has her super-supportive parents and her friends who go on tour with her. Lay Lay even chose her label because they felt like family. She knows how lucky she is to have so many people in her corner when things get tough.

Who do you go to when you have a problem? Is it a family member? A best friend? Someone at your school? Write their name here: _____

_____

What makes this person your person? _____

_____

How long have you known your person? _____

How did you meet? _____

_____

_____

Write a story about how you knew you wanted this person in your life. _____

_____

_____

_____

Write about a time that your person was there for you when life got hard—or a time when you were there for them. How did it feel having them in your corner?

One time, Lay Lay and her friends got into a huge water gun fight while on tour. They had to go onstage afterward soaking wet!

Have you and your friends ever done something crazy? What happened? Who else was there? What was so unforgettable about this time? Write all about this wild memory here!

"The advice that I have is to always keep going. If you have something that you really wanna do, then just do it."

Lay Lay has taken inspiration from a ton of things in her life. Make a list of things that inspire you here. This can be people you know, celebrities you admire, songs you love—anything that gets your creative juices flowing!

REMIX

A freestyle can be your opportunity to show the world what you've got and tell them what's up! Add your own remix verse to Lay Lay's song "Show N Tell" in the space below. Don't hold back—this is your moment to steal the spotlight!

"SHOW N TELL"

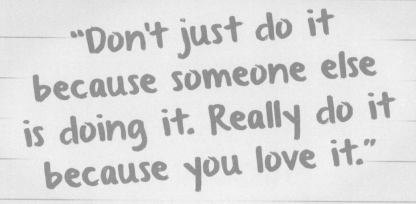

"Don't just do it
because someone else
is doing it. Really do it
because you love it."

What's the most important part of a song? Without lyrics, a beat is just keeping tempo. But without a beat to spit over, lyrics are just poetry. Are there any beats out there that you can't get out of your head? Maybe ones you think you could remix to make them even better than the original? Use this page to list the songs you think you could spit a dope freestyle over.

	TITLE	ARTIST
♥		
♥		
♥		
♥		
♥		
♥		
♥		
♥		

PLAY ♥

Pick your favorite song from the previous page and listen to it on repeat for a bit. Once you have a handle on the beat, use the lines below to draft a freestyle to create your very own remix. Next time you hear your song come up on shuffle, perform your collab for a crowd!

A big part of getting ready in the morning is making sure that every hair is in place before you start your day. You gotta make sure them edges are still poppin'! Use the space below to show us why you're *this* close to putting "Professional Celebrity Hair Stylist" on your résumé.

"That's the edges and I ain't even put nothin' on them. And they still poppin'!"

YOU CAN GET WITH THIS, OR YOU CAN GET WITH THAT

Even superstars like That Girl Lay Lay have to make tough choices sometimes. Read the options below and circle which *you* would prefer if you had to choose.

WOULD YOU RATHER . . .

Zak movies

Spend the day with your favorite movie star

OR

spend the day with your favorite rapper?

Have a small, tight squad

OR

a hundred casual friends?

Have your flight delayed

OR

lose your luggage?

Be the most talented member of a local band

OR

be the least talented member of a world-famous band?

Have a really big tour bus

OR

a really small private plane?

Be able to sing in any language

OR

be able to play any instrument?

Have to perform your big concert in the dark

OR

without any backup music?

Have the best vocals in your crew

OR

the tightest dance moves?

Lay Lay turned her love of rapping and performing into a successful career as a superstar!

What's something that you're really good at and would love to turn into a job one day? _____

_____

How do you think that you could get even better at that hobby and become one of the best of the best? _____

_____

_____

_____

How could you could use this skill to get big? For example, if you love making cookies, maybe you could hold a bake sale in your neighborhood or enter a local baking competition! Get creative — the best ideas come from out-of-the-box thinking!

_____

_____

_____

_____

"I feel like a microphone gives me, like, a burst of energy!"

> "A loss can motivate you, like 'I know I lost that time, but let me keep going and see if I can win the next time.'"

Lay Lay always knows how to keep going, even when something is hard or she doesn't get it right the first time. Have you ever had an experience where you had to try something over and over again before you got it right?

What motivates you to keep going in those moments? Write all about it here so you can read through these pages when times get tough!

Fashion, music, television, cosmetics . . . The sky's the limit for That Girl Lay Lay, so you never know where she might pop up next!

But what's next for *you*? Don't worry if you don't have it all figured out just yet. Take this quiz for some inspiration!

1. After a long day at school, who are you most excited to see?
A. I already miss the classroom
B. The people I live with
C. The warm glow of the TV screen
D. My bed, so I can spend some quality time *alone*!

2. Who recommended the last book you read?
A. A teacher assigned it
B. My best friend
C. I saw a celebrity reading it
D. I don't even know how I got *this* book

3. It's movie night! What're you watching?

A. A documentary about something educational

B. A comedy—it's fun for the whole family

C. Something artsy that won a lot of awards

D. It doesn't matter—I'm falling asleep during the trailers

4. You're in charge of dinner tonight. What's on the menu?

A. Something well researched and prepared

B. Grandma's family recipe

C. I'm going to wing it

D. We're ordering pizza!

5. Where can you be found at a party?

A. Chatting with my classmates

B. Hanging with my crew in the corner

C. Blaring karaoke, even if it isn't that kind of party

D. Wherever the pets are

6. Your class is doing show-and-tell. What are you bringing to share with the class?

A. A really cool geode you found outside

B. Your grandmother's antique teakettle

C. A copy of your favorite movie

D. Your pet turtle

MOSTLY As

You've got a curious mind! Your heart and mind are set on school at the moment, and that's an attitude that will get you far!

MOSTLY Bs

You're focused on family. Whether that's your parents, your siblings, or your crew and chosen family, you're always looking out for the people you love most.

MOSTLY Cs

You're practically ready for your close-up! You love the limelight and, even better, the limelight loves you back. Superstardom, here you come!

MOSTLY Ds

You're not quite sure where you're headed next, and that's okay, too! Whatever your next journey is, it's bound to be an adventure!

Motivation is what keeps us going even when things may not be fun or easy. What songs motivate you? What is it about them that inspires you to keep going? Use this page to create a playlist that makes you feel like you can take on the world.

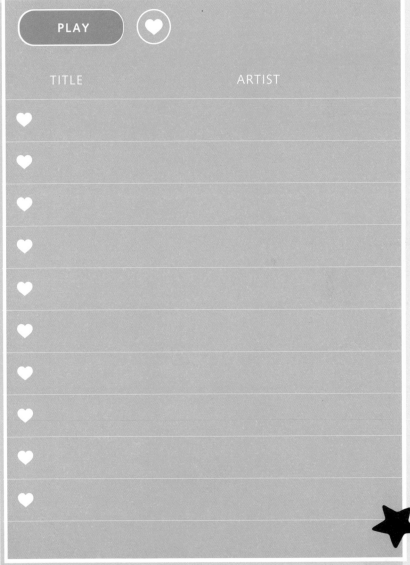

PLAY

TITLE   ARTIST

Lay Lay has always known that she was destined to be a star. But if you went back and told little Lay Lay what she would be doing now, even *her* mind would be blown! Think back to who you were years ago, months ago, even days ago, and write a letter to your past self telling them about your life now.

Dear Past Me,

Like a good freestyle, the future can be unpredictable. What do you think the future holds for you? Record deals? An award-winning TV show? A national tour? Write a letter to the person that you might become, and keep this book close so you can see which of your predictions come true!

Dear Future Me,

"You have to stay positive and leave all negative energy out."